MEETING OF THE BOARD

MEETING OF THE BOARD

by Alan E. Nourse

It was going to be a bad day. As he pushed his way nervously through the crowds toward the Exit Strip, Walter Towne turned the dismal prospect over and over in his mind. The potential gloominess of this particular day had descended upon him the instant the morning buzzer had gone off, making it even more tempting than usual just to roll over and forget about it all. Twenty minutes later, the water-douse came to drag him, drenched and gurgling, back to the cruel cold world. He had wolfed down his morning Koffee-Kup with one eye on the clock and one eye on his growing sense of impending crisis. And now, to make things just a trifle worse, he was going to be late again.

He struggled doggedly across the rumbling Exit strip toward the plant entrance. After all, he told himself, why should he be so upset? He *was* Vice President-in-Charge-of-Production of the Robling Titanium Corporation. What could they do to him, really? He had rehearsed *his* part many times, squaring his thin shoulders, looking the union boss straight in the eye and saying, "Now, see here, Torkleson—" But he knew, when the showdown came, that he wouldn't say any such thing. And this was the morning that the showdown would come.

Oh, not because of the *lateness*. Of course Bailey, the shop steward, would take his usual delight in bringing that up. But this seemed hardly worthy of concern this morning. The reports waiting on his desk were what worried him. The sales reports. The promotion-draw reports. The royalty reports. The anticipated dividend reports. Walter shook his head wearily. The shop steward was a goad, annoying, perhaps even infuriating, but tolerable. Torkleson was a different matter.

He pulled his worn overcoat down over frayed shirt sleeves, and tried vainly to straighten the celluloid collar that kept scooting his tie up under his ear. Once off the moving strip, he started up the Robling corridor toward the plant gate. Perhaps he would be fortunate. Maybe the reports would be late. Maybe his secretary's two neurones would fail to synapse this morning,

5

and she'd lose them altogether. And, as long as he was dreaming, maybe Bailey would break his neck on the way to work. He walked quickly past the workers' lounge, glancing in at the groups of men, arguing politics and checking the stock market reports before they changed from their neat gray business suits to their welding dungarees. Running up the stairs to the administrative wing, he paused outside the door to punch the time clock. 8:04. Damn. If only Bailey could be sick—

Bailey was not sick. The administrative offices were humming with frantic activity as Walter glanced down the rows of cubbyholes. In the middle of it all sat Bailey, in his black-and-yellow checkered tattersall, smoking a large cigar. His feet were planted on his desk top, but he hadn't started on his morning Western yet. He was busy glaring, first at the clock, then at Walter.

"Late again, I see," the shop steward growled.

Walter gulped. "Yes, sir. Just four minutes, this time, sir. You know those crowded strips—"

"So it's *just* four minutes now, eh?" Bailey's feet came down with a crash. "After last month's fine production record, you think four minutes doesn't matter, eh? Think just because you're a vice president it's all right to mosey in here whenever you feel like it." He glowered. "Well, this is three times this month you've been late, Towne. That's a demerit for each time, and you know what that means."

"You wouldn't count four minutes as a whole demerit!"

Bailey grinned. "Wouldn't I, now! You just add up your pay envelope on Friday. Ten cents an hour off for each demerit."

Walter sighed and shuffled back to his desk. Oh, well. It could have been worse. They might have fired him like poor Cartwright last month. He'd just *have* to listen to that morning buzzer.

The reports were on his desk. He picked them up warily. Maybe they wouldn't be so bad. He'd had more freedom this last month than before, maybe there'd been a policy change. Maybe Torkleson was gaining confidence in him. Maybe—

The reports were worse than he had ever dreamed.

"Towne!"

Walter jumped a foot. Bailey was putting down the visiphone receiver. His grin spread unpleasantly from ear to ear. "What have you been doing lately? Sabotaging the production line?"

"What's the trouble now?"

Bailey jerked a thumb significantly at the ceiling. "The boss wants to see you. And you'd better have the right answers, too. The boss seems to have a lot of questions."

Walter rose slowly from his seat. This was it, then. Torkleson had already seen the reports. He started for the door, his knees shaking.

It hadn't always been like this, he reflected miserably. Time was when things had been very different. It had *meant* something to be vice president of a huge industrial firm like Robling Titanium. A man could have had a fine house of his own, and a 'copter-car, and belong to the Country Club; maybe even have a cottage on a lake somewhere.

Walter could almost remember those days with Robling, before the switchover, before that black day when the exchange of ten little shares of stock had thrown the Robling Titanium Corporation into the hands of strange and unnatural owners.

*

The door was of heavy stained oak, with bold letters edged in gold:

TITANIUM WORKERS
OF AMERICA
Amalgamated Locals

MEETING OF THE BOARD

Daniel P. Torkleson, Secretary

The secretary flipped down the desk switch and eyed Walter with pity. "Mr. Torkleson will see you."

Walter pushed through the door into the long, handsome office. For an instant he felt a pang of nostalgia—the floor-to-ceiling windows looking out across the long buildings of the Robling plant, the pine paneling, the broad expanse of desk—

"Well? Don't just stand there. Shut the door and come over here." The man behind the desk hoisted his three hundred well-dressed pounds and glared at Walter from under flagrant eyebrows. Torkleson's whole body quivered as he slammed a sheaf of papers down on the desk. "Just what do you think you're doing with this company, Towne?"

Walter swallowed. "I'm production manager of the corporation."

"And just what does the production manager *do* all day?"

Walter reddened. "He organizes the work of the plant, establishes production lines, works with Promotion and Sales, integrates Research and Development, operates the planning machines."

"And you think you do a pretty good job of it, eh? Even asked for a raise last year!" Torkleson's voice was dangerous.

Walter spread his hands. "I do my best. I've been doing it for thirty years. I should know what I'm doing."

"*Then how do you explain these reports?*" Torkleson threw the heap of papers into Walter's arms, and paced up and down behind the desk. "*Look* at them! Sales at rock bottom. Receipts impossible. Big orders canceled. The worst reports in seven years, and you say you know your job!"

"I've been doing everything I could," Walter snapped. "Of course the reports are bad, they couldn't help but be. We

8

haven't met a production schedule in over two years. No plant can keep up production the way the men are working."

Torkleson's face darkened. He leaned forward slowly. "So it's the *men* now, is it? Go ahead. Tell me what's wrong with the men."

"Nothing's wrong with the men—if they'd only work. But they come in when they please, and leave when they please, and spend half their time changing and the other half on Koffee-Kup. No company could survive this. But that's only half of it—" Walter searched through the reports frantically. "This International Jet Transport account—they dropped us because we haven't had a new engine in six years. Why? Because Research and Development hasn't had any money for six years. What can two starved engineers and a second rate chemist drag out of an attic laboratory for competition in the titanium market?" Walter took a deep breath. "I've warned you time and again. Robling had built up accounts over the years with fine products and new models. But since the switchover seven years ago, you and your board have forced me to play the cheap products for the quick profit in order to give your men their dividends. Now the bottom's dropped out. We couldn't turn a quick profit on the big, important accounts, so we had to cancel them. If you had let me manage the company the way it should have been run—"

Torkleson had been slowly turning purple. Now he slammed his fist down on the desk. "We should just turn the company back to Management again, eh? Just let you have a free hand to rob us blind again. Well, it won't work, Towne. Not while I'm secretary of this union. We fought long and hard for control of this corporation, just the way all the other unions did. I know. I was through it all." He sat back smugly, his cheeks quivering with emotion. "You might say that I was a national leader in the movement. But I did it only for the men. The men want their

9

dividends. They own the stock, stock is supposed to pay dividends."

"But they're cutting their own throats," Walter wailed. "You can't build a company and make it grow the way I've been forced to run it."

"Details!" Torkleson snorted. "I don't care *how* the dividends come in. That's your job. My job is to report a dividend every six months to the men who own the stock, the men working on the production lines."

Walter nodded bitterly. "And every year the dividend has to be higher than the last, or you and your fat friends are likely to be thrown out of your jobs—right? No more steaks every night. No more private gold-plated Buicks for you boys. No more twenty-room mansions in Westchester. No more big game hunting in the Rockies. No, you don't have to know anything but how to whip a board meeting into a frenzy so they'll vote you into office again each year."

Torkleson's eyes glittered. His voice was very soft. "I've always liked you, Walter. So I'm going to pretend I didn't hear you." He paused, then continued. "But here on my desk is a small bit of white paper. Unless you have my signature on that paper on the first of next month, you are out of a job, on grounds of incompetence. And I will personally see that you go on every White list in the country."

Walter felt the fight go out of him like a dying wind. He knew what the White list meant. No job, anywhere, ever, in management. No chance, ever, to join a union. No more house, no more weekly pay envelope. He spread his hands weakly. "What do you want?" he asked.

"I want a production plan on my desk within twenty-four hours. A plan that will guarantee me a five per cent increase in dividends in the next six months. And you'd better move fast, because I'm not fooling."

*

Back in his cubbyhole downstairs, Walter stared hopelessly at the reports. He had known it would come to this sooner or later. They all knew it—Hendricks of Promotion, Pendleton of Sales, the whole managerial staff.

It was wrong, all the way down the line. Walter had fought it tooth and nail since the day Torkleson had installed the moose heads in Walter's old office, and moved him down to the cubbyhole, under Bailey's watchful eye. He had argued, and battled, and pleaded, and lost. He had watched the company deteriorate day by day. Now they blamed him, and threatened his job, and he was helpless to do anything about it.

He stared at the machines, clicking busily against the wall. An idea began to form in his head. Helpless?

Not quite. Not if the others could see it, go along with it. It was a repugnant idea. But there was one thing they could do that even Torkleson and his fat-jowled crew would understand.

They could go on strike.

*

"It's ridiculous," the lawyer spluttered, staring at the circle of men in the room. "How can I give you an opinion on the legality of the thing? There isn't any legal precedent that I know of." He mopped his bald head with a large white handkerchief. "There just hasn't *been* a case of a company's management striking against its own labor. It—it isn't done. Oh, there have been lockouts, but this isn't the same thing at all."

Walter nodded. "Well, we couldn't very well lock the men out, they own the plant. We were thinking more of a lock-*in* sort of thing." He turned to Paul Hendricks and the others. "We know how the machines operate. They don't. We also know that the data we keep in the machines is essential to running the business; the machines figure production quotas, organize blueprints, prepare distribution lists, test promotion

11

schemes. It would take an office full of managerial experts to handle even a single phase of the work without the machines."

The man at the window hissed, and Pendleton quickly snapped out the lights. They sat in darkness, hardly daring to breathe. Then: "Okay. Just the man next door coming home."

Pendleton sighed. "You're sure you didn't let them suspect anything, Walter? They wouldn't be watching the house?"

"I don't think so. And you all came alone, at different times." He nodded to the window guard, and turned back to the lawyer. "So we can't be sure of the legal end. You'd have to be on your toes."

"I still don't see how we could work it," Hendricks objected. His heavy face was wrinkled with worry. "Torkleson is no fool, and he has a lot of power in the National Association of Union Stockholders. All he'd need to do is ask for managers, and a dozen companies would throw them to him on loan. They'd be able to figure out the machine system and take over without losing a day."

"Not quite." Walter was grinning. "That's why I spoke of a lock-in. Before we leave, we throw the machines into feedback, every one of them. Lock them into reverberating circuits with a code sequence key. Then all they'll do is buzz and sputter until the feedback is broken with the key. And the key is our secret. It'll tie the Robling office into granny knots, and scabs won't be able to get any more data out of the machines than Torkleson could. With a lawyer to handle injunctions, we've got them strapped."

"For what?" asked the lawyer.

Walter turned on him sharply. "For new contracts. Contracts to let us manage the company the way it should be managed. If they won't do it, they won't get another Titanium product off their production lines for the rest of the year, and their dividends will *really* take a nosedive."

"That means you'll have to beat Torkleson," said Bates. "He'll never go along."

"Then he'll be left behind."

Hendricks stood up, brushing off his dungarees. "I'm with you, Walter. I've taken all of Torkleson that I want to. And I'm sick of the junk we've been trying to sell people."

The others nodded. Walter rubbed his hands together. "All right. Tomorrow we work as usual, until the noon whistle. When we go off for lunch, we throw the machines into lock-step. Then we just don't come back. But the big thing is to keep it quiet until the noon whistle." He turned to the lawyer. "Are you with us, Jeff?"

Jeff Bates shook his head sadly. "I'm with you. I don't know why, you haven't got a leg to stand on. But if you want to commit suicide, that's all right with me." He picked up his briefcase, and started for the door. "I'll have your contract demands by tomorrow," he grinned. "See you at the lynching."

They got down to the details of planning.

*

The news hit the afternoon telecasts the following day. Headlines screamed:

MANAGEMENT SABOTAGES ROBLING MACHINES
OFFICE STRIKERS THREATEN LABOR ECONOMY
ROBLING LOCK-IN CREATES PANDEMONIUM

There was a long, indignant statement from Daniel P. Torkleson, condemning Towne and his followers for "flagrant violation of management contracts and illegal fouling of managerial processes." Ben Starkey, President of the Board of American Steel, expressed "shock and regret"; the Amalgamated Buttonhole Makers held a mass meeting in protest, demanding that "the instigators of this unprecedented crime be permanently barred from positions in American Industry."

MEETING OF THE BOARD

In Washington, the nation's economists were more cautious in their views. Yes, it *was* an unprecedented action. Yes, there would undoubtedly be repercussions—many industries were having managerial troubles; but as for long term effects, it was difficult to say just at present.

On the Robling production lines the workmen blinked at each other, and at their machines, and wondered vaguely what it was all about.

Yet in all the upheaval, there was very little expression of surprise. Step by step, through the years, economists had been watching with wary eyes the growing movement toward union, control of industry. Even as far back as the '40's and '50's unions, finding themselves oppressed with the administration of growing sums of money—pension funds, welfare funds, medical insurance funds, accruing union dues—had begun investing in corporate stock. It was no news to them that money could make money. And what stock more logical to buy than stock in their own companies?

At first it had been a quiet movement. One by one the smaller firms had tottered, bled drier and drier by increasing production costs, increasing labor demands, and an ever-dwindling margin of profit. One by one they had seen their stocks tottering as they faced bankruptcy, only to be gobbled up by the one ready buyer with plenty of funds to buy with. At first, changes had been small and insignificant: boards of directors shifted; the men were paid higher wages and worked shorter hours; there were tighter management policies; and a little less money was spent on extras like Research and Development.

At first—until that fateful night when Daniel P. Torkleson of TWA and Jake Squill of Amalgamated Buttonhole Makers spent a long evening with beer and cigars in a hotel room, and floated the loan that threw steel to the unions. Oil had followed with hardly a fight, and as the unions began to feel their oats, the changes grew more radical.

Walter Towne remembered those stormy days well. The gradual undercutting of the managerial salaries, the tightening up of inter-union collusion to establish the infamous White list of Recalcitrant Managers. The shift from hourly wage to annual salary for the factory workers, and the change to the other pole for the managerial staff. And then, with creeping malignancy, the hungry howling of the union bosses for more and higher dividends, year after year, moving steadily toward the inevitable crisis.

Until Shop Steward Bailey suddenly found himself in charge of a dozen sputtering machines and an empty office.

*

Torkleson was waiting to see the shop steward when he came in next morning. The union boss's office was crowded with TV cameras, newsmen, and puzzled workmen. The floor was littered with piles of ominous-looking paper. Torkleson was shouting into a telephone, and three lawyers were shouting into Torkleson's ear. He spotted Bailey and waved him through the crowd into an inner office room. "Well? Did they get them fixed?"

Bailey spread his hands nervously. "The electronics boys have been at it since yesterday afternoon. Practically had the machines apart on the floor."

"I know that, stupid," Torkleson roared. "I ordered them there. Did they get the machines *fixed?*"

"Uh—well, no, as a matter of fact—"

"Well, *what's holding them up?*"

Bailey's face was a study in misery. "The machines just go in circles. The circuits are locked. They just reverberate."

"Then call American Electronics. Have them send down an expert crew."

Bailey shook his head. "They won't come."

"They *what?*"

"They said thanks, but no thanks. They don't want their fingers in this pie at all."

"Wait until I get O'Gilvy on the phone."

"It won't do any good, sir. They've got their own management troubles. They're scared silly of a sympathy strike."

The door burst open, and a lawyer stuck his head in. "What about those injunctions, Dan?"

"Get them moving," Torkleson howled. "They'll start those machines again, or I'll have them in jail so fast—" He turned back to Bailey. "What about the production lines?"

The shop steward's face lighted. "They slipped up, there. There was one program that hadn't been coded into the machines yet. Just a minor item, but it's a starter. We found it in Towne's desk, blueprints all ready, promotion all planned."

"Good, good," Torkleson breathed. "I have a directors' meeting right now, have to get the workers quieted down a bit. You put the program through, and give those electronics men three more hours to unsnarl this knot, or we throw them out of the union." He started for the door. "What were the blueprints for?"

"Trash cans," said Bailey. "Pure titanium-steel trash cans."

It took Robling Titanium approximately two days to convert its entire production line to titanium-steel trash cans. With the total resources of the giant plant behind the effort, production was phenomenal. In two more days the available markets were glutted. Within two weeks, at a conservative estimate, there would be a titanium-steel trash can for every man, woman, child, and hound dog on the North American continent. The jet engines, structural steels, tubing, and other pre-strike products piled up in the freight yards, their routing slips and order requisitions tied up in the reverberating machines.

But the machines continued to buzz and sputter.

The workers grew restive. From the first day, Towne and Hendricks and all the others had been picketing the plant, until angry crowds of workers had driven them off with shotguns. Then they came back in an old, weatherbeaten 'copter which hovered over the plant entrance carrying a banner with a plaintive message: ROBLING TITANIUM UNFAIR TO MANAGEMENT. Tomatoes were hurled, fists were shaken, but the 'copter remained.

The third day, Jeff Bates was served with an injunction ordering Towne to return to work. It was duly appealed, legal machinery began tying itself in knots, and the strikers still struck. By the fifth day there was a more serious note.

"You're going to have to appear, Walter. We can't dodge this one."

"When?"

"Tomorrow morning. And before a labor-rigged judge, too." The little lawyer paced his office nervously. "I don't like it. Torkleson's getting desperate. The workers are putting pressure on him."

Walter grinned. "Then Pendleton is doing a good job of selling."

"But you haven't got *time*," the lawyer wailed. "They'll have you in jail if you don't start the machines again. They may have you in jail if you *do* start them, too, but that's another bridge. Right now they want those machines going again."

"We'll see," said Walter. "What time tomorrow?"

"Ten o'clock." Bates looked up. "And don't try to skip. You be there, because *I* don't know what to tell them."

Walter was there a half hour early. Torkleson's legal staff glowered from across the room. The judge glowered from the bench. Walter closed his eyes with a little smile as the charges were read: "—breach of contract, malicious mischief, sabotage of the company's machines, conspiring to destroy the livelihood of ten thousand workers. Your Honor, we are preparing briefs to prove further that these men have formed a conspiracy to undermine the economy of the entire nation. We appeal to the spirit of orderly justice—"

Walter yawned as the words went on.

"Of course, if the defendant will waive his appeals against the previous injunctions, and will release the machines that were sabotaged, we will be happy to formally withdraw these charges."

There was a rustle of sound through the courtroom. His Honor turned to Jeff Bates. "Are you counsel for the defendant?"

"Yes, sir." Bates mopped his bald scalp. "The defendant pleads guilty to all counts."

The union lawyer dropped his glasses on the table with a crash. The judge stared. "Mr. Bates, if you plead guilty, you leave me no alternative—"

"—but to send me to jail," said Walter Towne. "Go ahead. Send me to jail. In fact, I *insist* upon going to jail."

The union lawyer's jaw sagged. There was a hurried conference. A recess was pleaded. Telephones buzzed. Then: "Your Honor, the plaintiff desires to withdraw all charges at this time."

"Objection," Bates exclaimed. "We've already pleaded."

"—feel sure that a settlement can be effected out of court—"

The case was thrown out on its ear.

And still the machines sputtered.

*

Back at the plant rumor had it that the machines were permanently gutted, and that the plant could never go back into production. Conflicting scuttlebutt suggested that persons high in uniondom had perpetrated the crisis deliberately, bullying Management into the strike for the sole purpose of cutting current dividends and selling stock to themselves cheaply. The rumors grew easier and easier to believe. The workers came to the plants in business suits, it was true, and lounged in the finest of lounges, and read the *Wall Street Journal*, and felt like stockholders. But to face facts, their salaries were not the highest. Deduct union dues, pension fees, medical insurance fees, and sundry other little items which had formerly been paid by well-to-do managements, and very little was left but the semi-annual dividend checks. And now the dividends were tottering.

Production lines slowed. There were daily brawls on the plant floor, in the lounge and locker rooms. Workers began joking about the trash cans; then the humor grew more and more remote. Finally, late in the afternoon of the eighth day, Bailey was once again in Torkleson's office.

"Well? Speak up! What's the beef this time?"

"Sir—the men—I mean, there's been some nasty talk. They're tired of making trash cans. No challenge in it. Anyway, the stock room is full, and the freight yard is full, and the last run of orders we sent out came back because nobody wants any more trash cans." Bailey shook his head. "The men won't swallow it any more. There's—well, there's been talk about having a board meeting."

Torkleson's ruddy cheeks paled. "Board meeting, huh?" He licked his heavy lips. "Now look, Bailey, we've always worked well together. I consider you a good friend of mine. You've got to get things under control. Tell the men we're making progress. Tell them Management is beginning to weaken from its original stand. Tell them we expect to have the strike broken in another few hours. Tell them anything."

He waited until Bailey was gone. Then, with a trembling hand he lifted the visiphone receiver. "Get me Walter Towne," he said.

MEETING OF THE BOARD

*

"I'm not an unreasonable man," Torkleson was saying miserably, waving his fat paws in the air as he paced back and forth in front of the spokesmen for the striking managers. "Perhaps we were a little demanding, I concede it! Overenthusiastic with our ownership, and all that. But I'm sure we can come to some agreement. A hike in wage scale is certainly within reason. Perhaps we can even arrange for better company houses."

Walter Towne stifled a yawn. "Perhaps you didn't understand us. The men are agitating for a meeting of the board of directors. We want to be at that meeting. That's the only thing we're interested in right now."

"But there wasn't anything about a board meeting in the contract your lawyer presented."

"I know, but you rejected that contract. So we tore it up. Anyway, we've changed our minds."

Torkleson sat down, his heavy cheeks quivering. "Gentlemen, be reasonable! I can guarantee you your jobs, even give you a free hand with the management. So the dividends won't be so large—the men will have to get used to that. That's it, we'll put it through at the next executive conference, give you—"

"The board meeting," Walter said gently. "That'll be enough for us."

The union boss swore and slammed his fist on the desk. "Walk out in front of those men after what you've done? You're fools! Well, I've given you your chance. You'll get your board meeting. But you'd better come armed. Because I know how to handle this kind of board meeting, and if I have anything to say about it, this one will end with a massacre."

*

The meeting was held in a huge auditorium in the Robling administration building. Since every member of the union

20

owned stock in the company, every member had the right to vote for members of the board of directors. But in the early days of the switchover, the idea of a board of directors smacked too strongly of the old system of corporate organization to suit the men. The solution had been simple, if a trifle ungainly. Everyone who owned stock in Robling Titanium was automatically a member of the board of directors, with Torkleson as chairman of the board. The stockholders numbered over ten thousand.

They were all present. They were packed in from the wall to the stage, and hanging from the rafters. They overflowed into the corridors. They jammed the lobby. Ten thousand men rose with a howl of anger when Walter Towne walked out on the stage. But they quieted down again as Dan Torkleson started to speak.

It was a masterful display of rabble-rousing. Torkleson paced the stage, his fat body shaking with agitation, pointing a chubby finger again and again at Walter Towne. He pranced and he ranted. He paused at just the right times for thunderous peals of applause.

"This morning in my office we offered to compromise with these jackals," he cried, "and they rejected compromise. Even at the cost of lowering dividends, of taking food from the mouths of your wives and children, we made our generous offers. They were rejected with scorn. These thieves have one desire in mind, my friends, to starve you all, and to destroy your company and your jobs. To every appeal they heartlessly refused to divulge the key to the lock-in. And now this man—the ringleader who keeps the key word buried in secrecy—has the temerity to ask an audience with you. You're angry men; you want to know the man to blame for our hardship."

He pointed to Towne with a flourish. "I give you your man. Do what you want with him."

MEETING OF THE BOARD

The hall exploded in angry thunder. The first wave of men rushed onto the stage as Walter stood up. A tomato whizzed past his ear and splattered against the wall. More men clambered up on the stage, shouting and shaking their fists.

Then somebody appeared with a rope.

Walter gave a sharp nod to the side of the stage. Abruptly the roar of the men was drowned in another sound—a soul-rending, teeth-grating, bone-rattling screech. The men froze, jaws sagging, eyes wide, hardly believing their ears. In the instant of silence as the factory whistle died away, Walter grabbed the microphone. "You want the code word to start the machines again? I'll give it to you before I sit down!"

The men stared at him, shuffling, a murmur rising. Torkleson burst to his feet. "It's a trick!" he howled. "Wait 'til you hear their price."

"We have no price, and no demands," said Walter Towne. "We will *give* you the code word, and we ask nothing in return but that you listen for sixty seconds." He glanced back at Torkleson, and then out to the crowd. "You men here are an electing body—right? You own this great plant and company, top to bottom—right? *You should all be rich*, because Robling could make you rich. But not one of you out there is rich. Only the fat ones on this stage are. But I'll tell you how *you* can be rich."

They listened. Not a peep came from the huge hall. Suddenly, Walter Towne was talking their language.

"You think that since you own the company, times have changed. Well, have they? Are you any better off than you were? Of course not. Because you haven't learned yet that oppression by either side leads to misery for both. You haven't learned moderation. And you never will, until you throw out the ones who have fought moderation right down to the last ditch. You know whom I mean. You know who's grown richer and richer since the switchover. Throw him out, and you too can be rich." He paused for a deep breath. "You want the code word to unlock the machines? All right, I'll give it to you."

He swung around to point a long finger at the fat man sitting there. "The code word is TORKLESON!"

*

Much later, Walter Towne and Jeff Bates pried the trophies off the wall of the big office. The lawyer shook his head sadly. "Pity about Dan Torkleson. Gruesome affair."

Walter nodded as he struggled down with a moose head. "Yes, a pity, but you know the boys when they get upset."

"I suppose so." The lawyer stopped to rest, panting. "Anyway, with the newly elected board of directors, things will be different for everybody. You took a long gamble."

"Not so long. Not when you knew what they wanted to hear. It just took a little timing."

"Still, I didn't think they'd elect you secretary of the union. It just doesn't figure."

Walter Towne chuckled. "Doesn't it? I don't know. Everything's been a little screwy since the switchover. And in a screwy world like this—" He shrugged, and tossed down the moose head. "*Anything* figures."